Hello, Family Members,

Learning to read is one of the most important accomplishments of early childhood. **Hello Reader!** books are designed to help children become skilled readers who like to read. Beginning readers learn to read by remembering frequently used words like "the," "is," and "and"; by using phonics skills to decode new words; and by interpreting picture and text clues. These books provide both the stories children enjoy and the structure they need to read fluently and independently. Here are suggestions for helping your child *before*, *during*, and *after* reading:

Before

- Look at the cover and pictures and have your child predict what the story is about.
- Read the story to your child.
- Encourage your child to chime in with familiar words and phrases.
- Echo read with your child by reading a line first and having your child read it after you do.

During

- Have your child think about a word he or she does not recognize right away. Provide hints such as "Let's see if we know the sounds" and "Have we read other words like this one?"
- Encourage your child to use phonics skills to sound out new words.
- Provide the word for your child when more assistance is needed so that he or she does not struggle and the experience of reading with you is a positive one.
- Encourage your child to have fun by reading with a lot of expression . . . like an actor!

After

- Have your child keep lists of interesting and favorite words.
- Encourage your child to read the books over and over again. Have him or her read to brothers, sisters, grandparents, and even teddy bears. Repeated readings develop confidence in young readers.
- Talk about the stories. Ask and answer questions. Share ideas about the funniest and most interesting characters and events in the stories.

I do hope that you and your child enjoy this book.

　　　　　　—Francie Alexander
　　　　　　Reading Specialist,
　　　　　　Scholastic's Learning Ventures

To Sarah and Jane,
with love
— M.L.

To Abby Normal, the singing dog
— M.D.R.

**Special thanks to Priscilla A. Lightcap, DVM,
of Fieldstone Veterinary Care for her expertise.**

ISBN 0-439-20542-5

Text copyright © 2001 by Melinda Luke.
Illustrations copyright © 2001 by Marcy Dunn Ramsey.
All rights reserved. Published by Scholastic Inc.
SCHOLASTIC, HELLO READER, CARTWHEEL BOOKS and associated logos are trademarks and/or registered trademarks of Scholastic Inc.

Library of Congress Cataloging-in-Publication Data
Luke, Melinda
      Helping paws : dogs that serve / by Melinda Luke ; illustrated by Marcy Dunn Ramsey.
            p.   cm. — (Hello reader! Level 4)
      ISBN 0-439-20542-5 (pbk.)
            1. Working dogs — Juvenile literature. [1. Working dogs. 2. Dogs.] I. Ramsey, Marcy Dunn, ill. II. Title. III. Series.
      SF428.2 .L85 2001
      636.7'0886 — dc21   00-036540

10 9 8 7 6   02 03 04 05

Printed in the U.S.A.   23
First printing, May 2001

HELPING
PAWS
DOGS THAT SERVE

by Melinda Luke
Illustrated by Marcy Dunn Ramsey

Hello Reader! — Level 4

SCHOLASTIC INC.
Cartwheel
·B·O·O·K·S·®

New York   Toronto   London   Auckland   Sydney
Mexico City   New Delhi   Hong Kong

Chapter One

A Dog Tale

Wolf Dog

Does your dog look like a wolf? Or act like a wolf? Probably not — yet all dogs are descended from wolves.

Over 12,000 years ago, prehistoric people began to tame and breed the wolves that lived around them. With each new generation, there were changes. After a while, many of these wolves did not even look or act like wolves. These were the first dogs.

Over the years, many dog breeds were developed. Today there are over 300 different types of dogs.

Dogs are part of the animal family Canidae. They are often called canines. Other branches of the Canidae family include wolves, jackals, coyotes, and foxes.

Dog Sense

Which of your senses do you use when you go to school? You *see* your friends, *hear* your teacher, *smell* your gym shoes, *touch* your desk, and *taste* your lunch. You use all five senses every day.

If you took your dog to school, it would *smell* your friends, your teacher, your gym shoes, your desk, and your lunch. Of course dogs use their other senses as well. But smell is as important to a dog as seeing and hearing are to you. Smell helps dogs recognize people, places, and animals.

Why is a dog's nose so much better than ours? Dog and human noses have special cells that receive scents. But dogs have about 40 times more scent-receiving cells in their noses than we do.

Sound

Dogs also have very good hearing. They can hear
sounds that are too distant or high-pitched for you to
hear. All dogs hear better than people. But dogs with
naturally upright ears hear best of all!

Sight

Can a dog see its own tail wagging when it is looking straight ahead? It depends on where its eyes are placed. For example, a cocker spaniel, with eyes on the front of its head, probably cannot see its tail. But a collie, with eyes on the sides of its face, can see all the way back to its tail.

Dogs cannot see colors or details clearly. But they are much better than humans are at spotting motion. For instance, a dog may see a bird moving around in the branches of a tree better than it sees each leaf on the tree.

Dogs and People

Wolf and dog packs are like human families. The oldest male and oldest female are in charge and tell the younger ones what to do. Domestic dogs think their human families *are* their pack. This makes dogs easy to live with and train.

Instinct

A mother dog carries her pups gently in her mouth. A dog who is not hungry buries a bone for a later meal. A sled dog digs down into the snow to keep warm. How do they know to do these things without being taught? All dogs are born with natural **instincts**: knowledge and behavior that is unlearned.

But dogs can learn new skills, too, from catching a ball to pulling a wheelchair. Their desire to learn new tasks makes them perfect for many jobs.

Chapter Two
Working Dogs

Hunting Dogs

Hunters, ranchers, and farmers use dogs to help them in their work. Dogs have natural hunting instincts. They herd and drive prey toward other members of their "pack family."

Hounds find game and move it into the open where the hunter waits. Retrievers are used for fetching game, such as birds. Terriers follow game underground. For thousands of years, dogs have helped people feed their families.

Herding Dogs

A shepherd and his dog are a team. The shepherd whistles to send the Border collie into a field of sheep. The dog circles around and stops a distance from the flock. The shepherd whistles again. The dog comes toward the sheep and begins to move them. Now the sheep are running. The dog glares at the sheep. The sheep are afraid. They will do what the dog tells them. By whistle and voice commands, the shepherd tells the dog where to move the sheep.

The sheep trot into a pen. *That'll do,* says the shepherd. For now, the dog's work is done. Panting, the dog flops down. The dog will rest until the next time its master says, *See sheep?*

Dogs are used for moving and protecting herds of livestock. Herding dogs are smart and love to work.

Many countries have their own breeds of sheep and cattle dogs. Border collies, sheepdogs, collies, shepherds, corgis, and the Australian cattle dog are some of the best-known animals that work livestock.

Some of these dogs are popular as family pets. Often, the herding instincts are so strong that the dog will herd small children or other pets.

corgi

English
sheepdog

German
shepherd

Shetland
sheepdog

collie

Border
collie

Dog Power

For many years in some parts of the world, dog power was just as popular as horsepower and ox power — and much cheaper! In Europe, long before the gasoline engine was invented, dogs pulled carts for people selling their wares.

Before there were horses in North America, dogs helped Native Americans drag their belongings from camp to camp on **travois** poles.

Where ice and snow cover the ground much of the time, dogsleds were used for local transportation and racing. They were also used for expeditions to the North and South poles. Samoyeds, huskies, and malamutes are breeds that are comfortable living in cold climates and good at pulling sleds. And today, dog teams and sleds are still used in one of the most famous annual sled races in the world — the 1,200-mile Alaskan Iditarod!

Chapter Three

Brave Hearts

Canine Cops

What makes a great police officer? Bravery. Intelligence. Loyalty. Hard work. Honesty. No wonder dogs serve on the police force, too!

Police officers get their dogs as puppies and raise them as part of their families. When the dog is 18 months old, the officer and dog begin their formal training. After several months, the dog and officer graduate. The canine cop is a patrol dog. Throughout their careers, the officer and dog spend one day per month in more training. The canine cop will live its entire life with its officer. The dog usually retires from police duty when it is eight or nine years old.

Police Academy

Obedience training for a police dog begins with simple voice commands: *Come. Sit. Stay. Down. Heel.* Dogs learn to walk on and off a leash.

Then they begin agility training. Special obstacle courses help them get used to working in strange places. For example, dogs learn not to be fearful of dark spaces by training in canvas tunnels. They learn to balance and walk on moving surfaces by training on seesaws.

Police dogs are also taught to growl and attack on command. They learn ways to catch and hold a fleeing suspect. Dogs are trained in tracking the smell of humans: in the air, on the ground, and even as it rises off the water.

Many of the dogs are also trained in other forms of police work, such as finding drugs or explosives.

Dogs are helpful in finding things that may have been used to commit a crime, such as weapons. Police dogs can search a building or a large outdoor area faster than human police officers. They also protect their human partner. Controlling an angry person or a crowd is much easier when police dogs are present. And because police work is dangerous, dogs even have their own, specially made, bullet-proof vests!

War Dogs

Since ancient Egyptian and Roman times, dogs have
served in wars. Their instincts — keen senses, the
desire to protect their "pack," and the ability to
fight — have served us well on battlefields.

Military dogs receive basic obedience and agility
training. But they learn hand and arm signals as
well as voice commands, because a voice command
could alert the enemy as well as the dog.

Military dogs perform many jobs in war. They are
sentries on guard duty, alerting their handlers to
strangers or attacking on command. Combat units
patrol with scout dogs that silently signal that the
enemy is near.

Military dogs save lives in many ways. Scout dogs try to find traps, land mines, trip wires, and explosives before anyone gets hurt. Messenger dogs carry coded messages, medicine, or equipment over battlefields that no person could cross. Casualty and rescue dogs find the wounded wherever they have fallen. Dogs have bravely served behind enemy lines — doing work that is too dangerous for people. Remarkably, some have been trained to parachute into enemy territory to complete their life-saving missions.

Search-and-Rescue Dogs

When natural disasters occur, many things are destroyed. Earthquakes turn buildings into rubble. Hurricanes and tornadoes blow homes apart. Rising floodwaters wash away houses, cars, and people. Bombs explode and buildings collapse.

When disasters like these occur, search-and-rescue teams of handlers and dogs are often among the first to help. They assist rescue workers, police, firefighters, and medical teams.

The training of search-and-rescue dogs begins with obedience and agility. Next they learn many ways to find lost, trapped, or injured people. Search-and-rescue dogs are trained to pick up scents in the air and on the ground. Sometimes they will use a piece of clothing to help them find a certain person, such as a missing child.

Search-and-rescue dogs search through collapsed buildings. They signal rescue workers when they find a victim. Some of these dogs wear a specially fitted head collar. It has a video camera, light, and microphone. As the brave dog makes its way toward a victim, rescue workers can watch on video monitors. They can see exactly what the dog is seeing. This helps rescue teams make good choices about the safest ways to rescue victims. It also helps doctors to be ready with the right medical treatments.

CHAPTER FOUR

Service Dogs

Guide Dogs

In 1928, a German shepherd named Buddy became the first Seeing Eye dog. People discovered that dogs could provide services to people who are blind or deaf. Today, people with many special needs have easier lives because of Buddy and dogs like her.

When dogs began to work in service roles, many public places would not let them inside. Restaurants refused to serve blind customers who arrived with a guide dog. Trains and buses would not let the dogs board. Office buildings refused to admit guide dogs.

The Americans with Disabilities Act (ADA) changed that. The ADA is a law that makes it illegal to treat someone differently because he or she is disabled. Now people with a guide or service animal can go anywhere other people can go. They do not have to prove that they need their animal.

Guide dogs spend their first year living with a foster family. They are house-trained and taught basic manners. Guide dogs should not be nervous around strangers or in public places, so their foster families take them everywhere! When they are about a year old it is time for the future guide dog to go to school. It must say good-bye to its foster family.

Like most dog training, guide work starts with simple obedience. Some of the commands that are important for guide dogs are: *Sit. Stay. Come. Down. Forward. Right. Left.* Dogs need to learn to wear the U-shaped harness that the owner will hold.

Agility training is important, too. Dogs need
to learn to lead their owners. They must make
decisions. It is their job to keep their owners safe.
Sometimes it is their job to say *No!* to their owners.
For instance, a blind person may give the command
Forward! But if the dog sees something dangerous, it
must refuse the command and find a way around the
problem. Not every dog can do this. Many dogs begin
guide-dog school, but not all of them will graduate.
Only the best dogs can become someone's eyes.

After the guide dog has finished its training, it is time for it to meet its human companion. This is an exciting time for a person who is blind or can't see well. It can be a little scary, too. Many blind people are used to having other people help them. It may be frightening to put their trust in a dog instead.

Guide dog trainers need to train the blind person, too. They need to teach the commands and how to care for the dog. Both the dog and the new owner need to get used to each other.

Hearing Dogs

What is an **alert**? It is a signal that a dog gives in response to a certain sound or event.

Dogs who bark when the doorbell rings are performing a service. They are alerting their family to someone's arrival. Now, imagine you are deaf. You cannot hear the doorbell — or the barking dog. A "hearing dog" has other ways to alert you to the doorbell. And that is just what it is trained to do! Here is how it works:

The doorbell rings. The hearing dog realizes it is the front door. The dog runs all through the house, looking for its owner. It finds the owner unpacking groceries in the kitchen. The dog sits and gently nudges the owner's leg. The owner knows this is an alert. She signals or asks, *Where?* The dog quickly leads the owner back to the front door. This may sound simple. But by the time the owner reaches the front door, the person ringing the doorbell may have gone away.

Hearing dogs have to be very energetic. They also have to be calm enough to deal with many sounds happening at once. From the moment the alarm clock goes off in the morning, the dog will have work to do. Think of all the things you hear in a day: the telephone, doorbell, timers, your spoken name, the whistling teapot, a siren on the street, a smoke detector, the approach of a stranger. A hearing dog works very hard. It listens for its owner twenty-four hours a day, seven days a week.

Even good hearing dogs can develop problems. Just like people, dogs can get bored. They can get tired of fetching their owners every time the doorbell rings or the alarm clock buzzes. They can get lazy, too. Training can "wear off" when no one corrects a hearing dog's mistakes. And a deaf person might never know that his or her dog did not alert. Again, it takes a special dog to be someone's ears!

Canine Assistants

Not all disabled people need a dog to be their eyes and ears. Some disabled people just need a dog to do the laundry.

People with certain diseases are often weak. Some are in wheelchairs. Even with help from human caregivers, everyday life can be very difficult.

Canine assistants are there to help! These dogs can be trained to turn on lights, pull a wheelchair, and get things that are dropped or out of reach. They can open and close drawers — and yes, even put clothes in the washer and take them out of the dryer!

Some people need extra help balancing themselves. Having a dog to lean on can keep them from falling. Someone who uses a cane or a walker may find it hard to carry anything. Getting around a busy city can be especially difficult, but an assistance dog can carry a bag. The dog can also protect its owner from being bumped on the street or on public transportation.

Canine assistants can help in other ways, too. For people in constant pain or those recovering from an accident, having a dog can be a distraction from their own problems. They focus on the dog instead of on themselves.

Having an assistance dog can bring an extra bonus. Owners get attention from other people because of their wonderful dog instead of their wheelchair or disability.

Seizure Dogs

All service dogs are special. But some are extra special. Some can do things they haven't been trained to do. For example, a dog may be able to alert its owner that an epileptic seizure is coming. People who suffer from seizure disorder often do not know that a seizure is about to happen. With warning, they can go to a safe place and get help. The warning helps them avoid hurting themselves.

Sadly, no one knows how these dogs sense that a seizure is coming. That is why this skill cannot be trained in service dogs.

Therapy Dogs

Dogs make most people feel better. Whether dogs visit a school, a hospital, a nursing home, or the neighbors, they make people happy.

A therapy dog can be any breed, any age, or any size. It must be calm, well mannered, and willing to be touched by strangers. The best therapy dogs seem to know instinctively who needs them.

Therapy dogs visit schools for children who have learning or behavior problems. Therapy dogs also help children return to school after an episode of school violence. The dogs come to school each day and visit until the students feel safe again.

Nursing homes often use therapy dogs. Many older people become sad when they go to live in a nursing home. Many have medical problems and feel lonely. Residents pet the dogs or let them sit on their beds. Often the dogs remind an older person of the pets they used to have. It may have been a long time since someone held the resident's hand or hugged them. Dogs love to be petted and to cuddle with older people. Many people look forward each week to the dog visits.

Hospitals are starting to use therapy dogs, too. Severely ill people seem to improve after a therapy dog visits them. Doctors can measure the improvement in heart rates and blood pressure.

Remarkable dogs are all around us. They offer
a warm heart and helping paw to those who need
them. They see and hear for us when we cannot.
They help us get well when we are sick. They
comfort us when we are frightened. They find us
when we are lost. And they risk their lives to protect
us when we are in danger. These remarkable dogs
are miracles with paws!